Teddy's Game

By
SM Russell

Chapter One

"You put us in a cage!" Arbogast was indignant and addled, but the gun never wavered. It stayed there, level, aimed right at Teddy's heart. "You led us into a world where we have no choice."

Teddy looked around. The Oval Office of the President of the United States, his office. The pieces of furniture in the room were hundreds of years old, all of them. "They've heard stories like this," he thought, "watched as old men like me and young men like him thought through this very problem." Ever closer to the desk, he creeped.

"Stop!" Arbogast cried.

Teddy froze.

Arbogast slammed his free hand down on the desk, "Why? That's what I want to know. Why did you do it?"

"Why did I do what?" Teddy said, hands raising slowly.

"Why did you create this...this world around us?"

"*I* created? I created..." Teddy shook his head, "You know, there were several times *we* could've turned back from this destiny. Do you really think the rest of the world had no agency?"

Arbogast spit on the floor. It landed on the leg of an antique sofa, slid down the leg until it was absorbed by deep blue carpet. "You say you didn't create the world we live in, but you must know I know better. You put all the pieces together."

"And so have you, apparently," Teddy mused, "all but one."

Arbogast refocused his weapon and prepared to fire. "Wait!" Teddy shouted, "You wanted to know the why. I'll tell you. I'll tell you the why, the how, all of it. We can talk and then you can decide whether this death sentence is appropriate."

Arbogast felt the weight of the gun in his hand. It felt strong, decisive. It felt like all the things this world was not. There were few guns, these days, and almost none of them loaded. It was a privilege to hold such a firm decision in his hand. And he knew his decision: he wanted to know. He knew he would be asked, on the off chance he survived long enough to get back to his handlers. He knew History would want to know. Would Theodore Redhed really tell him?

Teddy watched the wheels turn in Arbogast's head, anticipating his doubt he said, "I've built my life on fact...on good, solid information. You must know that if you're standing here about to kill me. You've done your research. Why would I end my life with a lie?"

Arbogast sneered, "You'd say anything to walk away."

Teddy straightened, then said matter-of-factly, "Am I going to be walking away?"

Arbogast stared back at him. It was true...there was no way out for President Teddy Redhed, not now. Still, "You will play for time until someone comes in."

"You know you picked the best time to come here. You know I work late and that I value solitude in the evenings as it's the time I use to get most things done. You know you've got until that gun goes off and attracts the guards."

And Arbogast knew that was true too. He'd seen Teddy's private schedule. He'd picked this time for exactly one reason: he wanted this answer. He knew, in his heart, that he wanted the answer.

"And anyway," Teddy continued, "I have a question I want to ask you in return. I will give you an answer and in return you can answer me."

"What possible question could you have to ask of your murderer?" Arbogast did his best to make it sound sinister.

"What's so wrong about this world that you would kill the one you blame for bringing it into being?"

Suddenly Arbogast winced with anger. His blood boiled. He felt his sweaty finger fondle the hair trigger. The gun would go off and he would be done with it all. Then...he calmed.

Redhead was right, of course. Arbogast had time. All night if they were both quiet enough not to disturb the guards. He would get his answer. And he would give his answer too, for all the good it would do Teddy. This silver tongue dog had had his day. Arbogast made sure of that when he walked in. Quietly, Arbogast gestured with his gun for Teddy to sit in the plush chair in front of the desk. Arbogast cautiously took the seat across from him. Between them, a long wooden coffee table, the wood finely varnished, looked as though it was built before factories. "You. You first," he said, never once taking his eyes or the gun from Teddy.

"Fine by me." Teddy said as he relaxed onto the chair.

"Hands where I can see them at all times, understood? Or I might not get to hear the end of your story." Arbogast cast the barrel of the gun over Teddy's body.

"No tricks. I'm going to do what I've always done. I'm going to tell you the truth." Teddy said.

"Be brief." Arbogast said.

Teddy looked indignant, "*You* asked me why. Let me tell you! It's a lifetime in the experiencing, so it'll take a little time in the telling."

Chapter Two

Teddy settled in and began.

"Of course, life here on Earth was going to shit a long time before the pandemic. We had destroyed most of the environment, alienated whole segments of the planet's population with casual racism and economic laziness, and let our technology get the better of our minds with streams of always-on internet media crowding out independent thought.

We tried to build (out of fear of the human condition, of all things) a world where humans could interface with the world entirely as consumers. Life as a Service...that was the dream. And it did us a lot of good too, I might add. Most of the amenities you enjoy today were developed back then. Cell phones, streaming services, instant shipping, service drones, self-driving transportation, weather regulators...all developed prior to the pandemic, although some these days would have had you believe otherwise.

Still, our processes were wasteful and isolating. We were a petty culture that used people to achieve petty ends and, when we were done, we threw away whatever we'd wasted, people and materials, into the sea or the gutter or the landfill. This, of course, caused the environmental crises of the early parts of our century.

But before that, it caused the pandemic.

All this you know. What you don't know is that, while a displaced Wuhan bat was making its way into the dinner of some poor unlucky farmer, I was working at Sa-Data Solutions as a business consultant. Before you ask, a business consultant means I told businesses what to do about certain things. My expertise, and the expertise of my company, was data. Sa-Data told businesses how to get the most out of their data and, let me assure you, the businesses needed the help.

Businesses, from the global banks and governments all the way down to the local beer microbrewery, were looking to understand their customers, their market, and the world better. This would help them make better products, present better marketing campaigns, and grow their business.

The best example I can think of now is a self-driving car company we advised. They were looking to roll out a self-driving fleet of vehicles and were trying to pull together a business case that a high-profile test market couldn't refuse. We were looking at traffic data from just one city, San Francisco. Back then, of course, people still mostly drove themselves around. Nothing was scheduled and nothing was coordinated so people waited their turn for other people to go ahead of them or, more often, people *wouldn't* wait their turn and instead try to get where they were going just a little bit faster than everyone else. This often led to what was politely called traffic jams, or gridlock, where the cars get backed up on the roads and no one goes anywhere.

The company we were supporting collected all the data from all the street cameras in the whole of this great big city for just one year. That's 24 hours of interactions for something like 15,000 cameras, for 365 days per year. Imagine trying to track down and identify every car that drove through just your hometown for just yesterday. Now imagine also needing to know the drivers of those cars, the reports of how the cars have been driven in the past, whether or not the drivers in the cars were law breakers that day or in the past, how the traffic was flowing that day, which intersections were busy, which bypasses were underutilized, how many vehicles were public transport, how many were commercial, which were...it exhausts me just talking about it.

I wonder if anyone then, if anyone now, thinks about how much information is readily available on them at any given moment.

Anyway, we computers for what they're designed to do, and let them look at all this data, training them to pull out patterns. I worked with a team of solutions architects who helped businesses curate and interpret their data using, among other things, artificial intelligence algorithms.

That is, I did, until the pandemic.

Once it hit, corporations started to circle the wagons. Some customers just decided to stop paying us, others were gracious enough to let us run out our contracts. Still, within 4 months, I was without work, without pay and facing inflation that threatened to wipe out what little savings I had.

I realized, in that moment, how completely attached to this economy I had been. I was a remora, sucking on the side of the shark's mouth, waiting for a morsel of food. It was a slap in the face for me. I felt hollow. I did a lot of soul searching back then. For a little while, there was a time when I was going to be a wildlife photographer? No kidding, I was really lost. But I was also lost in a world that was going to shit so fast, it seemed none of us could get a grip on it.

The world had finally decided to stop accepting all the punishment we'd been doling out and had started doling out punishments of its own in the form of flooding and insane heat waves, the people had elected madmen or weaklings to leadership positions in key areas around the world and so nothing was getting done, the people were at odds with each other due to the universal misinformation that was and still is the internet.

If I was lost, I had plenty of company.

I decided, as the new year finally ticked over, that I was going to do something about it. I thought I might complete a charity half marathon or give blood. What ended up happening was quite different.

What happened? I got a call from an old friend, from my consulting days. She had been mulling the data over from the customer I told you about, the one that monitored traffic. She told me she'd found something...something I should see.

Chapter Three

"It was still dangerous to go outside in those days, but that wasn't stopping everyone. A whole group of discontented pandemic deniers were going around, licking things they wouldn't have touched with their fingers before someone told them they might get sick. I saw a group of these types coming my way as I got out of my car.

As I crossed the street to Rana's apartment complex one of them got up in my face. He made to spit, and I shied away. He let out a roaring laugh and screamed to his friends "You see? He's afraid of the sick! Fucking sheep, man." I felt the cold sweat creep up the back of my neck as I watched the man bouncing around with his friends. They were all big...like they worked construction at one of those sites where no one was legally able to operate heavy machinery, so everything was done with massive hand tools.

The confrontation had legitimately scared me. I was worried about getting spit on. I was worried about getting sick, also, though not that worried. I'd had the sickness, you see, but I was one of the lucky ones that got better. I felt like I had a natural immunity...despite evidence to the contrary, I might add. I guess we all walk around with our own fictions.

More than the fear of illness, I was afraid of their largeness, their hardened muscles, their power. They were enormous and angry and ignorant. I always found that a frightening combination. They could've killed me with their bare hands and, in those days, it felt like they just might.

I tried to shake it off as Rana buzzed me upstairs. The elevator had been recently cleaned and the smell of bleach was overwhelming. It didn't end there, as cleaners were bleaching the walls and windowsills in the hallway. I rushed past and headed to the door. Rana was waiting for me with white plastic gloves, a face shield and a mask. "Rana, you have those glasses on, you don't need a face shield."

"You know how it is," she said, "an ounce of prevention...prevents things. Now turn around, I have to mist you."

"What?"

"Here, 0.01% solution of bleach. Not enough to be dangerous to your clothing, do not worry, but it will be quite deadly to anything you might've picked up from those dinosaurs I saw you messing with outside," she said.

"I just got out of your bleached down hallway, I'm not about to smell like bleach for the rest of the day," I protested.

"It's the price of admission, I am afraid," she said, "but I promise you, when you see what I have to show you, you won't be thinking about bleach."

Reluctantly, I put my arms out and turned around. She sprayed me down as I turned toward her and was nice enough to miss my head and most of my neck.

"Ok, come on in. Please leave your shoes outside though."

I removed my shoes and walked in. She had a nice place. Not for the first time, I wished I'd gotten into the development side rather than the business end. It seemed like there was never a time when developers didn't make money. I looked out the window, down on a water feature in the middle of a park built just for the residents. "So, what is it you needed me to come out and see?"

Rana sat down at her computer. "It's here. Remember that customer we had? The one with all the traffic data?"

"Yeah, yeah...I was just thinking about them the other day actually," I said.

In fact, I had been on their website looking for jobs I might apply for. It had gotten pretty bad. Rana continued, "When we were working for them on their traffic analysis algorithms, I felt like I was missing something as I was testing the effectiveness of the AI. It was there, I knew it was there. It was on the edge of my consciousness, but I couldn't quite figure it out."

"Where is this going?" I asked.

"I made a copy of the data, so I could review it later. I just got back to it now, have been so busy with freelance work."

"Must be nice," I thought.

"When I reviewed the data with fresh eyes. I saw the pattern...I knew I needed you." She sounded suddenly very grave. "You must help me with this, Teddy."

"With what?" I said.

"Look here."

I watched as she clicked her mouse and objects on the screen kicked into motion. This was the test program we used. The map represented a 5 square mile radius in San Francisco. Each widget within the map was a simulated car, truck, bicycle, or pedestrian. The idea was to build a digital twin of the traffic patterns for a sample area within San Francisco. Then, we made the widgets as real as possible using information gathered from drivers' records, credit organizations, data brokers, etc. They were digital representations of real-world people, with likes and dislikes, preferences and styles, destinations, timelines, habits, fears, and loves. We watched the screen as they moved.

I'd seen it before. The algorithm was accounting for and predicting where each individual would go next, how they would achieve this (drive fast, wait too long at red lights, ogle attractive pedestrians, take their eyes off the road to give a rude gesture to an aggressive driver, etc.) and fed their predictions into an analyst subroutine. This would, in turn, help a self-driving car adapt to traffic patterns and leverage a networked algorithm to determine the best and safest routes. A machine learning tool would also monitor changes over time and build trend analysis which, would help improve the AI and help designers work with civil engineers on the future of roads. It was impressive stuff, really, but nothing new. "I've seen all this before," I said.

"Yes. This you've seen. But then I went to work for a medical company who wanted some AI."

"Oh?"

"It was a company looking to use AI/ML to identify new strains of genetic disorder and determine the appropriate DNA to synthesize and place into a CRSPR vector to deliver to a host."

"They're doing that now?" I said.

"The really, really rich are...if it works on them, we'll get it later I bet," she said. I chuckled and she went on. "This kickstarted something in my brain which took me right back to the algorithms you're seeing now. The AI/ML used a behavioral study model to identify the genetic expressions and determine the appropriate treatment. I realized that, if I used a variant of the AI/ML used in the CRSPR process, I could add the capability to the traffic model as an advertising tool. I thought, maybe if I provided the behavioral information of the drivers and trained the ML on advertising, I might be able to get somewhere." she pasted some code into the pad and little orange blocks appeared in the streets, representing road signs. "Then...I gave the AI/ML a problem to solve and the information from the driver sims: I wanted it to make sure no one took Fremont Street."

"That's the main road here." I said, pointing to the large line down the center of the map.

"I know. Watch." She typed in a few strings and executed.

In a few seconds, Fremont Street started to clear.

My mouth dried out. Then "It...it could've said road closed...right?"

"It didn't," she said, "the road sign said "It's time to visit him. You need to."

"What do you mean? Visit who?"

"I don't know, Ted." Rana was smiling staring at the screen as cars pulled off of Fremont left and right.

"What's the time factor?" I asked, thinking that she might have it set to a high-speed playback.

She nodded, "One second real-time equals 15 minutes in the model."

"No!" I said, that was way too fast.

"You can check for yourself if you want," she said, unable to contain the excitement in her voice.

"I...this can't be what I think it is. You..."I
stared in amazement as the realization started
to dawn on me. It knew.
Somehow, the algorithm, it knew. "This is...this
is going to change the world."
Rana held her hand to her mouth, then "You
see why I needed you. How shall we proceed?"

Chapter Four

"CRSPR is, at its heart, just a genetic sequence found in bacteria. For some reason, some bacteria evolved a mechanism to turn off targeted parts of DNA. Isn't that amazing? It does this by using a sequence of information injected into its system and then looking for matching sequence.

Rana had smartened it up further by providing an intelligent front end that could not only look through a vast library, but also draw conclusions about new combinations. And now, he had put that same front end, along with a digital vector, to work on the people in the model. But, of course, they were only people in a model.

"We need to test this," I said, "we need to see if this works on actual people."

"We need more than that, Teddy," Rana replied, "we need a way to get the message to the people."

"Right."

In the weeks that followed, I worked on the vector. What I came up with was what everyone has come to know of as The Boards. At first, The Boards were a simple flat rectangular LCD screen designed to give people the message. I thought that might be enough, but I wondered if the novelty of a computer monitor telling you something that might appear nonsense would be unsettling to the process of getting you to act.

The answer to that was to go subliminal. Working with Rana, I built an image generator that obfuscated the letters of the message somewhat. The result was that the message got through, sat at the edge of your consciousness. Meanwhile you were seeing a picture of nature. Why nature? Didn't I tell you I wanted to be a wildlife photographer?

Finally, we had a set of prototypes built and loaded with a version of the algorithm that Rana built. The Boards were born.

But still untested. We needed someone, someone who would be too small time to embarrass us if we failed, but someone who had definite contact with an unfamiliar end user. We needed to take The Boards as far away from California as possible. And I knew just the person to help us.

Chapter Five

The air was wet. Orlando, Florida and Los Angeles, California are both sunny, both hot. The difference? Humidity...swampy, muggy humidity. It's why everyone wears those shirts that make them look like retirees even when they've just graduated high school.

"Vin, I'm telling you, no cost to you at all," I said, "Just let us try out our software and, if you see some real results, I'll ask you for a positive recommendation, maybe a couple of quotes for the website."

Vincent Trong was the proud franchisee of no fewer than three Texron gas station and convenience stores. I stood there with Rana beside me, both of us sweating through our Hawaiian shirts, trying to convince Vin there wasn't anything wrong with my offer. So why wasn't this guy listening to me? Well, because our former company had litigated him for nonpayment, that's why. He owed a massive debt to the company and thought we were trying to bait him into some weird sting.

"You," he sneered, "You say you aren't with Sa-Data, but you consultants lie. You lie all day long!" His accent was a mix of Bronx and Nashville and made everything coming out of his mouth sound like a complaint from a cowboy.

"I'm telling you, look around. It's a pandemic. Call Sa-Data and ask to be put through to me. They'll tell you I'm not employed there."

"You are trying to get my money!"

"Vin, listen, I've got paperwork right here. If you want, I'll call a notary and we can get it witnessed by a neutral third party. I just want to test run our new algorithm. Look at us...we're sweaty, we're tired. For Christ's sake, I live in Los Angeles...do you see us coming out here if don't really need it? I need your help Vin, really. Will you help us?"

Vin paused, he looked from me to Rana, back to me. "Then I get the algorithm."

"No, Vin," I sighed, "We get the algorithm...but you...you get all the benefits for your business for 6 months! You can't do better than free."

Vin sighed, "How do I know this is for real?"

"I'll call the notary right now. I gave you my business card, check the company out on the internet. We're a real company."

Vin looked at the business card. We'd only just had them printed the week before. He sighed, exasperated. "I am ready to say no to you," he said, "but when I realize that we have been able to have this entire conversation in the middle of the afternoon without anyone interrupting us to buy something, I don't know what to say." He looked out at his pumps, all empty.

"Say yes," I pushed, "at the very least, customers will think it's weird to have screens like ours up. That'll probably give you a little boost, even if our new algorithm doesn't work."

Vin smiled, "I keep...The Boards."

I looked at Rana, she nodded. "Deal, Vin, we keep the algorithm, but you get The Boards we put up in your store. To celebrate, I'll buy us a round of beers from the cooler over there, oh and Rana'll fill up on 6."

The first time someone saw The Boards was in a convenience store on Mitchum Hammond Road. It was a group of four migrant workers actually, who'd come in for an energy drink. The camera did its work, and the database was scanned.

Not much found on this group, just a driving record for one of them, some small-time criminal activity for three of them, kids too soon and marriage too late for one (when cross referenced with the age of his kids and his wife). The sign had been told to sell something people didn't usually buy: White Chocolate. We'd placed the white chocolate in eyeshot of all The Boards, so it was hard to miss.

Now, when was the last time you had a bar of white chocolate? Statistically only about one in ten people can stomach a bar of white chocolate. This was an extreme test and, unfortunately, our test subjects ranked in the very least likely to want a bar of white chocolate.

The sign spoke to them in Spanish. It said, well I don't speak Spanish but, in English, it said "Your mother's rose is sweet and pure. You need to honor her."

That was the first time The Boards had communicated to real human beings. And that was what they said.

That might have been all they said...except two of the four workers bought white chocolate bars. My heart threatened to jump out of my chest. As people filtered in, they bought white chocolate, whatever else they needed.

The message changed each time. A woman came in with her kids and read "The little bitch deserves to die in sugar." Sale. An old man came in, "Remember Easter in Bushwick?" Sale. A doctor looking for a pack of non-filters "She died, don't you feel anything about that?" Sale.

I honestly didn't stop to check if we broke a record for white chocolate sales in one day... but it didn't matter. We had something.

Over the next 6 months, we stress tested everything from buying top shelf liquor to buying a gas can and extra gas. Every single time, The Boards made sure the customers bought.

At last, we told Vin we were going to earn our keep, for real. For the last month, we tested sending customers away to bring in more business. This test doubly important to us. It represented a test of timing: how long would The Boards influence a viewer after having seen a message? Also, it was a test of The Board's ability to influence an abstract concept. Up until now, we'd been testing the ability to sell a directly available product. Selling the concept of a store, especially something as ubiquitous as a fueling station and convenience store, as something worthy of praise and recommendation was a whole different class of challenge. Was there a threshold for peoples' ability to be influenced by The Boards?

A young woman came in and bought some cigarette rolling papers. The sign simply said "this place is *safe*." Well, you guessed by now I'm sure, it was exactly what she needed to know. She came back that evening with three of her friends. They bought as much liquor and cigarettes as they could afford. The parking lot smelled of weed for the next couple of weeks, though.

He enjoyed the increased sales but, after one of the new customers was arrested in the parking lot for an open container liquor violation, Vin asked that we try to dissuade certain demographics while encouraging others. That turned out to be a great innovation and soon, we had The Boards selecting for demographic before delivering messages.

Over the course of the month, Vin's business at all three locations quadrupled. The Boards were having a significant effect. And, for the most part, the customer was the kind Vin needed: quiet, reasonably sober for Florida, and pleasant.

Our hit rates were between 40 and 60 percent. Then it was over. We took the algorithm, headed back to California, took out a business loan and opened the doors on our business: Isiah Inc.

Chapter Six

Isiah Inc. was an ATM. What we pitched: a little
Vin style proof of concept followed by a full-
blown engagement. It was irresistible.
Companies had never seen anything like The
Boards. After six months, you couldn't walk into
a major retailer or chain restaurant in Los
Angeles without seeing them. Even concerts had
them up, with indie music companies pushing
drinks, merchandise, anything that would get
the customer to drop a tenner in the bucket.
For Rana and me, the money was coming in.
But then, like the man said, it's no trick to
make a lot of money if all you want to do is
make a lot of money.
The issues we faced back then...climate,
polarizing politics, kids shooting up
schools...still went on, still escalated.
You don't know...couldn't know how much it
was everyone's problem. To think that, any
moment, our world could wipe us out because
of our addiction to sugar, or beef, or plastics. It
was too much for any of us to wrap our heads
around. It remained safely outside our scope of
thought, from a professional perspective
anyway, until one afternoon in July.
We were sitting in the outside patio of a
Kindlatte on Sherman Oaks Blvd in that part of
the San Fernando Valley where B-list television
stars hung out with summer stock "that-guys".
I was talking to Rana about what a massive
responsibility we've taken on and that it would
be difficult to bring people into the organization
in any real way. I felt we needed to be extra
careful not to open The Boards up to misuse. I
didn't want some political extremist to be able

to manipulate people in any way other than the limited commercial ways for which we'd been contracted.

It was already a point of pride that we didn't lease ourselves out to the political parties or to hate groups or to news media outlets (in those days all three might've meant the same thing). We contracted only with commercial clients that sold legal and generally helpful products. No guns, no vice beyond an extra beer at the family dinner spot. We'd gotten rich helping people sell clothes, food, vacations, and electric cars.

Rana needed the help, we were the only ones able to develop solutions, but she agreed that there wasn't anyone else she'd trusted with this, not yet anyway. I leaned in with my coffee cup and toasted her. That's when the shots rang out.

We hit the deck and I could feel hot coffee burn my legs. Clouds of latte foam streamed past my eyes as I tried desperately to figure out where the shots were coming from. I heard the twang of a ricochet and realized they were shooting in our direction. I looked over at Rana, safe but shocked. I tapped her arm and signaled her to follow me as I crawled toward the door of the coffee shop.

The megaphone was somehow attached to speakers they had mounted on the lead truck...some overengineered monster truck with tractor tires. Big body, no brains, like the dinosaurs. The goon on the megaphone identified the group of terrorists as Alt-Right Now, and they were letting the Hollywood liberal elite know that they were "touchable".

I crawled on my belly, keeping as low as I could but heading for the door of the Kindlatte.

I tried to quietly pull open the door with my fingers, but they were wet and I couldn't get a hold of the bottom corner without slipping. Megaphone went on about how they won't be silenced, no matter who was in office. That they were everywhere. That they were the police, the city councilmen, the schoolteachers. They let out another volley. Screams all hushed when the sound stopped. All but one. A woman, from the sound. She screamed and screamed.

"Must've been hit" I thought.

As soon as the shooting stopped, I slowly raised my hand to open the door. The firing continued. I lowered my hand immediately and braced as the broken glass fell on my head and back.

Megaphone said "You cower on the floor a little longer. That way you learn your place."

Rana stood up. She started walking toward the speaker. I was blinded with fear for my friend and partner, or I would've noticed she was limping. She'd been hit.

Megaphone was not amused. "Here. See? This is entitlement coming toward me. Well no one's gonna bail you out here!" Megaphone aimed a revolver at Rana's head, who still walked slowly toward him, muttering something inaudible under her breath.

I got up and tackled her, covering her as she hit the ground.

"Not here! Not here...we can't." I whispered.

"I can't," she said, struggling, "My grandfather..." she was in shock.

"You're not going to do any good. You'll only get killed," I hissed. I looked around at the terrorists, looking to see if they were about to open fire. They were looking to Megaphone.

Megaphone cleared his throat. For whatever reason, he'd lost interest in us. He went on. "I want all you to go back to all your fairy Hollywood friends and tell them. Tell them what you witnessed here today. Tell them that it's coming. We're coming for them, and if you think you're immune, we're coming for you too! This isn't their country, it's not your country, it's our country! And we aren't about to let you turn it into a filthy, house of sin!" He sat back down. I could see him clearly now. He was older than I was, but not by much. He looked like one of those muscle beach types, really. He was wearing a bandana, a muscle fit top, and a grin that seemed to indicate he was pleased with the way all this had gone down.

"Come on," he said, and he drove off with the rest of his entourage. Jeeps, maybe four or five, and two large vans sped off as the police sirens could be heard distantly wailing their approach. I got off of Rana and realized she was bleeding profusely from her left leg. She was angry at me and was about to yell we both heard, "the screams...that woman."

I helped her up and we limped over together. It was there, at that moment, when our lives...when Isiah Inc. when all of this...changed forever.

We looked down. The woman's screams ended in choked tears that drew the breath from our lungs. In her hands, like a broken heart, she held two large pieces of her daughter's skull.

Chapter Seven

It had been a couple of weeks, so I was surprised when I got the call from Rana to swing by.

I brought a bottle of some red wine, she liked red, as a peace offering. I wasn't sure if she was still mad at me for stopping her. Also...I needed a friend.

I hadn't slept well since that day in Sherman Oaks. Day and night, the vision of that little girl. I thought about how her mother will never be able to recover from what happened. I thought that it was right of Rana to be angry with me...I had enabled those thugs. I had cowered and worse, I forced her to cower.

So, I stood in a pool of sweat and emotion when I knocked on the door. My heart dropped through my stomach while I listened to her crutch thud slowly on the floor. When she opened the door, I could only look at the floor. I started into a practiced speech on how sorry I was. She didn't let me finish, "Come in! Come in! You have to see." She said as she pulled me in.

"Rana, Rana I'm so sorry, I..." she was pushing me with her free hand toward the computer. It took her a moment to hear me but then he stopped.

"You are sorry?" She said.

"Yes, Rana...my god. I pulled you down. You were standing up to those men...those men that killed..."

"My friend. You saved my life. I don't know what was going on with me. I owe you my life. And, more than that, I owe you for inspiring what I'm about to show you." She began pulling me over toward his computer. "Is that red wine? You should've brought champagne!" she said.

Rana settled into a seat behind her keyboard, "Now...you were right...I couldn't have fought back there. But...But I can fight back. We can fight back. Look."

She typed in the command. I won't bore you with code. She told the algorithm: Stop people from believing in a liberal conspiracy without hard evidence.

The algorithm went to work. The environment was an apartment complex in Orange County. This was one of the local demographics we were using to research a clothing retailer's attempts to sell more head scarves to suburban women. The Alt-Right groups would've been heavy there. Well, the algorithm worked, but we weren't getting nearly the response we were seeing with other prompts. "I don't get it," I said, "we're seeing a response but not nearly as high..."

"Exactly," Rana said, "but look at the profiles of the right-wing demographics we're not reaching. They all have one thing in common."

"Heavy internet use."

"Yes," she smiled, "someone's put a "Board", of sorts, in front of them first."

I shook my head, "Well, what are you showing me?"

"The Alt Right Now movement is using, albeit unwittingly, a version of our technology to push people into believing that filth they want to peddle."

"Right..." I turned toward the window. I was tired...exhausted. Seeing her not angry with me had given me permission to let my own feelings bottom out my energy levels. I couldn't figure out what she was trying to say. "What do we do with this information though? We can't sue them, can we?"

"No, no, no," Rana said, impatient, "don't you see? This is how we fight back! If we worked our way in, built virtual boards, we could make them irrelevant. We could take over their own websites and sour the milk without them even realizing what's happening. We could end the whole alt-right movement before it causes any more harm."

I stared at her for a moment. I thought I must be hearing her wrong. Finally, "I'm not sure...I mean, what you're saying. You're talking about influencing people to adjust their political beliefs."

"Not people," she roared, "Criminals, terrorists!" she softened, "The little girl..."

"I know..." I said.

"Then you can't tell me that you think we should walk away...when there's hope to stop that from ever happening again," she said.

I looked out of her window, down on the beautifully manicured private garden. By then, I had a view to rival it in Santa Monica, overlooking the Pacific and the Santa Monica Mountains. I thought about the little girl's mother and how she was in some Encino suburban box. "She'll never recover," I thought, "and meanwhile, we sit here in our ivory towers playing chess with peoples' minds."

"No," I said, "the thought's appealing. But the risk is too great. We are dealing with forces that could be turned to a very evil purpose. Imagine if the algorithm ever got out. We'd be paving the way for...for God knows what."

"And, while you sit there, making a decision not to help, who is paving our way for us?" She pointed to the screen, "How is it out there these days?"

I sighed. It was undeniable. The police seemed to arrive too late everywhere. It was clear that the Alt Right Now had secured their absence. And the politicians did what we all expected, took both sides depending on which audience was listening and quietly did nothing.

This thing, this monstrous new form of ignorance and anger, was growing, like a disease festering. "What do you want me to say? That the world isn't perfect? That it's worse this time? That I'm not sure if not acting is the right answer?"

Rana looked out the window, "I'm saying I'm going to act. I didn't invite you here to decide for me. I invited you here because I thought you deserved to know and because you, of all people, are the one I trust to make sure I don't go too far. I need someone, Teddy, someone I can trust."

I was tired, see and more than just because I couldn't sleep. I was exhausted of living in a world where people were looking for a backward revolution. I wanted to be proud and happy and feel safe again. Mostly, I think I just wanted to get that girl's blood off my hands. But we find possibilities in guilt. That's an overlooked advantage to guilt, I suppose, and I saw the chance to build a new and more stable world...for the first time, I saw what The Boards could *really* do. I also thought I could see how much damage they could do if they fell into the wrong hands. "If, *if* I helped you...this can't be about revenge," I said, "it'd need to be about building a better world."

Rana looked pensive for a moment, then "Agreed."

"What do we need to start?" I asked.

"Data...we need lots and lots of data."

Chapter Eight

We worked, took every contract we could stomach, opened factories in China and Mexico, employed thousands to manufacture more and more of The Boards. Business was booming, partly because guaranteed customer increase is a license to print money, but also because we were putting The Boards up everywhere you could look; on highways, in doctors' offices, in schools and universities, and designing virtual Boards for online advertising. We were anywhere capitalism would let us go...and that meant we were pretty much everywhere. Soon, you couldn't wake your phone without seeing one of our messages. Couldn't drive down the street without passing a Board. California, then the West, then the rest of America, then Europe, then Asia, then Africa. Even North Korea, after some tactful assistance from the US Government, allowed The Boards in their state buildings. I think they wanted to show that they were as modern as everyone else. As a matter of fact, I know that's what they wanted.

Of course, you won't remember that they were once an existential threat to the globe, peddling disinformation, nuclear weapons, and funding evil plots...now they're rich from selling rice and beer to most of Asia and selling cheap memorabilia of the dictator days to tourists. Anyway, we spent capital like crazy, built an empire of Boards. But we didn't do it for profit, we did it for reach. We started programming messages that support a balanced and rational view of the world. This was the dream, our dream. We would use our success in Isiah to fund a consciousness shift toward the center, toward reason, toward general respect for human life and decency.

It was a miracle of innovation, truly, even though I do say so myself. The Boards on the roadway, for example, would flip messages fast enough for each person to see the most effective message for them. Sometimes hundreds per minute. They would adjust as traffic increased and slow their role as it dissipated. As their presence grew, we saw an exponential jump in influence.

Online, it was even easier. One person looking at their phone got the same or complementary messages across each site they visited thanks to cookie tracking.

And the effect...the effect was incredible, but only in certain areas and only with certain demographics. We weren't reaching everyone. This had the effect of pacifying certain zones but creating additional friction in others.

We started to worry we may have inadvertently caused harm. The powder keg was filling up. Rana had been right of course. We weren't getting through because we didn't know the people we were trying to get through to. No database, no matter how vast the company's reach, could give us dependable information about every demographic.

Almost no database.

Companies didn't keep information on all types of people in all types of situations because no company built a product that was universally accepted by all. Governments, on the other hand, kept information on everyone, and we knew of one program in particular that represented the motherlode: The PRISM Surveillance Program.

This initially top-secret surveillance program tracked the phones, spending habits, online search trends and other obtainable information about anyone and everyone they could. It was uncovered in 2007 and, when it was discovered, the people were told it was necessary for National Security and that the data set was so large that no one could parse it.

Even then, that was a lie. Still, they hadn't done anything particularly useful with the data by the time we decided we needed to get access to it. But it was impossible to access it the way we needed to without one of two things happening: we either needed to be the contractor in charge of storing and maintaining the database, or one of us needed to be the President of the United States.

Needless to say, the first option was preferrable. We bought a data storage contracting company, got the appropriate committee to open up bidding on the contract and made ourselves the lowest bidder.

There we were, sitting in one of those offices with the dark wooden walls. We were across from House Appropriations Committee chairman and veteran Congressman from the great state of Mississippi, Maxwell Broad. He was a church going man and proudly displayed the etched glass award he'd received from his church for supporting Gay Conversion therapy. What a prick. Some people can't be told.

"Exactly what am I looking at here?" he said.

"Is the offer too high, Congressman?"

He laughed, "It's the lowest offer I've ever seen. How do you intend to do the job, boy? This is chicken feed."

I smiled, "Listen, I'm new to the business. We bought this company only a little while ago and we realize that we are the new kids on the block. As such...a discount to get stable business sounded like a really good idea to us. It's a win-win!"

He looked us over, then burst out laughing, "And you think that makes you the solid contender, right?"

"Well, as a taxpayer, I think I'd want my government to give contracts out for good work at a good price."

His eyes became narrow slits as he feigned an analytical eye, "You just said you're the new kid on the block...what guarantee do we have that you do good work?"

"That," I paused, then, "is a really good point." I thought for a moment. "I guess, if I were in a non-top-secret business, I'd tell you I'd do a proof of concept for you, show you our stuff."

"Yeah, well that's not going to help you much here, boy. I can't hand you information that's supposed to be code word clearance."

Rana piped up, "What about non-classified government information. We could build you an email management system. Would solve those problems government can have with their emails getting hacked or found out. Would that work?"

The Congressman sat back for a moment, looking at the two people in front of him. His nose whistled as he breathed patiently, in and out, for a full minute before speaking again. Then, finally, "You really are new to all this, aren't you? I mean, you get Los Angeles, maybe, and you get New York, maybe...but, boy, you've got a lot to learn if you want to rub two sticks together on the beltway. You know why I brought you here to my office to talk to you in person?"

"I can't imagine," I said, sensing what was coming.

"You have the, what do you call 'em, Boards. How come you never sell to politics?"

"It's a powerful tool, Congressman. We don't want to unfairly advantage a candidate."

"Yeah, well..." he sucked his teeth (I hate that), "you're gonna swim in the water with the rest of us if you wanna do business."

"What do you mean?" Rana asked.

"If you want this contract, I need The Boards. I need you to make all them little people vote my way."

"You want us to help you get re-elected?"

He laughed heartily, "The great state of Mississippi put me in this chair 16 years ago and they'll gladly *keep* me in this chair for 16 more. Honest to God, I never thought I'd have to tell you to think bigger. It's the prezzydentia next year!" he shouted with a big grin and, just at that moment, I realized there was some grease on the chin of his fat face. He went on and it glinted in the light, "Maxy's gonna make himself a little run for the big chair!"

"You want us to help you win the presidency?" Rana asked, trying and failing to keep the disbelief out of her voice.

"Look I can see I'm not getting through, and I've got a roll call in about 15 so keep quiet and listen. I'm going to lay it on the line for you. You don't get that contract. Not this time around. Even if I tried to get it for you, those boys vote for tried and tested people who've demonstrated loyalty and commitment and the ability to deliver in a top-secret situation time and again. That's why the contracts go for millions more than you've asked for. I'm not going to be able to help you now but if you work them little Boards for me. You might just get me president. Then we can talk about all kinds of nice, stable government contracts that will keep you in microchips and online porn for decades. You digging what I'm throwing down?"

I nodded silently...there was absolutely no way we were going to help this guy become president.

He left, thankfully, without shaking our hands.

I turned to Rana, "Looks like it's plan B."

Chapter Nine

It was a business decision, plain and simple.
One of us had to be president, and the most
logical choice was me. I was already the
spokesman of our company and, as Rana was
the stronger developer, she needed to be on-
sight reviewing the data and configuring The
Boards.

Now I look back on it and it was an incredibly
short period for making such a monumental
decision. Over the course of a week, I went from
being tech businessman Ted to Candidate for
President Teddy.

We started our campaign in Los Angeles, where
we already had a strong Board presence and
built out from there. Pretty soon, you couldn't
go 10 feet without seeing a Ted for President
sign or banner or commercial.

On the surface, we weren't different from any
other campaign...better funded perhaps...as we
had the deep pockets of many of our customers.
No, the secret wasn't our brand or our war
chest, it was that all the signs and
advertisements and banners were just a baffle.
The Boards were doing the real work. You see,
we inserted messages into The Boards of all our
clients, on all the digital Boards we bought for
the highways, online, everywhere we had reach.
You absolutely could not avoid us. I wish I
could say we put up Boards that influenced
people to care more about climate change or to
improve public schooling...but politics is a filthy
business...and it has always been easier to tear
down than it has been to build up. We fought
through the primary by inciting discomfort and
disdain for the other candidates. One actually

dropped out of the race, it was rumored, because she didn't feel like she would make a good president. We'd obviously got the message across.

By the time the primary rolled around, we were the strongest republican ticket by far. The general was even easier.

You see, it wasn't the best ideas. It wasn't enlightened debate. It was Commerce. It was who had the best ad agency. Who could reach the most people, change or nudge the most minds?

We were everywhere...everywhere it counted in an election year. In the end, it was too easy. And that bothered me, still bothers me.

I was raised to be an American, you see. I believed in its ideals. I still do, as a matter of fact. I believed so deeply. I suppose I thought I was heading for the end of the rainbow. We would run for President; we would see that our discovered algorithm had its limitations and then we would go home and spend our millions in relative anonymity.

You know that's not what happened.

I wish there was some vignette I could tell you now, about how close it got. I wish there was a moment when we were almost out of the race. That it was close. That we needed to redesign our applications for each market, that it took round the clock attention. It didn't.

I won the election with 70% of the popular vote and 74% of the electorate. I mean...not since Reagan had something like this happened. People who'd never voted in their lives, which was most of America at the time, had voted for me by the millions. The man I was running against, his daughter voted for me...she put it online.

I was swept on a wave of goodwill into an office that, months ago, I'd only ever thought I'd see on television.

Rana took over day to day operations of Isiah Inc. and we got the keys to PRISM, the biggest prize we could've hoped for. She moved in immediately and started work and so, I suppose, did I.

As soon as I was sworn in, I was the highest executive power in the Western World, empowered with the most powerful tools for directed change ever created. There were decisions to make.

Of course, at this point in the story, I thought being the president was going to be decisive in itself. Somehow, it still hadn't dawned on me that all the perceived power of any government was just so much fluff compared to the ability to move the minds of the people it governed. The real power, the key to every kingdom, was sitting in the servers within that mountain storage facility.

And when we finally tapped in, it was more than we could imagine.

We found data from virtually every country. Phone transcripts going back much farther than had previously been revealed to the public. Text messages, emails, web browsing history, purchases, digital tower records which would allow us to track movements en masse to within 2 feet. It was a gold mine.

Rana got to work ingesting data for what would be a decade long job. Meanwhile, I got to work building out the list of things we wanted to change.

The people were at the top of the list and the root of the problem, or so we thought. In the end, it wasn't the people, really. When you dug deeper, you could see the truth: we'd somehow built ourselves out of our own society.

The funny thing is, we spent an inordinate amount of time in those days worrying that we'd build some crazy machine that would evolve beyond us and lay waste to us in its wake. I guess we give power to the things we fear. Turns out, that's exactly what we were doing, but not a machine fed by artificial intelligence and no conscience; rather, we built a global network of economies, all powered by natural intelligence and most, if not all, lacking the conscience that most of us are both saved and plagued by.

We built a world to accelerate progress and, in the end, progress ran right over us. And no *one* was to blame.

The internet, a window into which we could see anything we wanted and we, like pitiful Narcissus, could find nothing more beautiful to gaze at then our own opinions, our own joys, our own fears, our own images. And our adversary, the high concepts we'd invented to govern this world of progress, exploited our addiction to provide grist for the mill. We were, all of us, little happiness machines, running around looking for happiness, looking no further than our phones, and finding only brief spasms of pleasure. And no *one* was to blame. But now there was a new player. We had the tools to use the machine the world built *conscientiously*. We could change humanity, allowing them to adapt and evolve beyond the rectangular boxes they'd unknowingly built around themselves.

That was the goal, nudge people into thinking they needed to understand the perspective of the other side. Nudge people toward taking a more peaceful approach toward solving problems and toward favoring people who did the same. Nudge people into behaviors that were outgoing, rather than introspective. Nudge people into communities and away from isolation. Environment over convenience; love over fear; the goal was to get people to prefer happiness to pleasure.

Do this well, we thought, and the rest would fall into place. And we would be to blame. And, right or wrong, we would have to face the consequences. Because, if there's no one to blame, we tend not to fix the problem.

Of course, there's another side to this story. There's your side for example. You're here, gun in hand, looking for the why before you put me down. And you're not alone, in fact you're in good company. Rana grew to share your concerns.

Chapter Ten

It was around the time I was using the algorithm to get people behind my plan to rescind the two-term limit.

See, when Rana and I made our plan, 8 years looked like more than enough time to make the changes. 6 years in, I could see things weren't going to be nearly where we thought they were. In fact, I estimated it would take 25 years to really make the impact we'd planned.

We had work to do, and I wasn't about to be interrupted by some antiquated laws.

Rana saw this as a reach into self-delusion.

Meanwhile, The Boards we had built were installed practically everywhere. Schools had them, even nurseries. Workplaces had them, as did religious places. Everyone wanted a piece. The nation, then the world. And we had data on them all. Everywhere we went, we were the power in the shadows. People thought of Isiah Inc. as the power behind the throne and, mostly, we were happy to let them think that way.

We did change the minds of the people. We were preparing them better for the mental onslaught of the internet and the modern world. We were nudging them toward tolerance and toward a love of learning. We nudged them toward the value of perspective and an understanding of the rarity of truth. And even these small steps were beginning to have a massive impact.

For one, the job of championing legislation became a breeze. We were able to pass laws, global charters and even new taxes for protecting the environment, building up the educational system, reprioritizing military, and reprioritizing exploration. We were able to create a demand for investigative journalism and reduce the demand for reality television.

People started to take a longer view. The world, their children, their nations, their species and others, seemed to matter again.

This was what we had hoped would happen, but I started to realize it wasn't enough.

This is where the need for longevity became apparent. It took five years, my whole first term and a year of my second, to ingest and fully configure the data in the model. This meant that all the victories we had were partial, albeit much better than we could've had before we had access to any PRISM data. If we were going to see this through, we needed more time. We could see it through. We just needed to hang on to power.

Now, I realize how that sounds. So did Rana. But if we just hung on for a bit longer, we could do what needed to be done. We could make a better world and have that world last. We could make people better, more ready.

Rana saw it differently. She felt that, whatever we might have gone into this to get, the temptation to play too much with the minds of the people had to be resisted and the temptation to alter the trajectory of the nation by changing a federal institution like the two-term limit was when she decided to make her concerns known.

"I'm not going to let you go down that road, Ted."

"I'm not talking about seizing military power or anything, just making it possible to continue making the difference we wanted to make. Look, you've seen the math. You understand that, if we walk away from it now, our children will inherit the world we lived in just 8 years ago, Boards or not."

"I have seen the math," she shouted, "you know how long you'd have to remain president to affect the kind of change you're talking about? 25 years!"

"It's the hand we were dealt," I said.

She chuckled, "No, it's the honeypot you're grabbing for. You've turned this into a crusade. No, that's not fair. We did this together. But think about where this is going. In 25 years, you'll have reduced people to nodes! They won't be able to think without The Boards."

"I can't accept that. The mind isn't so simplistic. How can you think that? And remember, everything we've done, we've done together."

Rana smiled, "Yes. Yes we have. And now I'm pulling the plug. I am going to destroy the algorithm," Rana softened, "Ted, we got into this to change minds and help our world become a better, safer place. We've done it. Anything more would be hubris. Anything more would be tyrannical. That's not you, that's not me. We've made our money and we've made great change. I think it's enough."

She was my best friend. I knew her and, in this mood, there was no talking her down. So, she really meant to destroy it. Destroy the creation that had brought us this far, the discovery that tempted belief we may in-fact hold the key to the next step in human evolution.

You make a decision like this once in your life. I told her that I would think about what she said, that she should too. If we still felt this way, then we should make a plan but, yes, destroy the algorithm. I pointed out that an uncontrolled draw down might have unintended consequences. She thanked me, told me that he knew that, of all people, I was the only man she knew capable of walking away from such an enormous temptation. My head spun out of control.

You make a decision like this once in your life. There was no one around. There was no one to see. She thanked me as she turned and pulled on her coat.

The decision was made before I'd really thought about it. My hand felt slid the server out of its cradle and it came crashing down on her head faster than I could make a decision. She was down but not unconscious. I hit her again. She was crawling forward, just trying to get away. I hit her again. This time she stopped moving. I tasted metal in my mouth. Sweat. I dragged her to an elevator shaft that was out of use. I can still taste that metal in my mouth now. It's adrenaline, they say.

They found her there, a week later, after I had reported her missing. She had apparently jumped down an elevator shaft and had died from massive injuries to the neck and head. Apparently. And that's the story that was published.

So, I sit here now, telling you the unvarnished story of my life and I want you to know, Arbogast, I want you to know that I killed her. I killed my best friend. I killed Rana that night and tossed her body down the shaft.

I don't...excuse me...I don't think I ever got over that moment. It was a decision I made.

I took a person's life, not just a person, but my friend. Not just my friend but a friend to the whole world, who invented something incredible, and decided to use it to help people as well as herself and me. I stood there, peering down into the blackness. I saw the mother, then, from Sherman Oaks Blvd. I remembered her weeping over her daughter's body. I wept. I wept and wept for Rana and for my poisoned soul.

But then, the next day, I committed to the task. I would not allow Rana's death to be in vain. I would dedicate my life to avoiding her warning. I would stay in power, all 25 years, and I would make a world and a people Rana would be proud of, without turning them into dependent automatons.

Chapter Eleven

It was not difficult to change the rules now. The boards nudged people into asking themselves a crucial question, on a subconscious level: Is it worth giving up prosperity now for an idealized version of a world where power passes on to an unknown quantity? My bill removing term limits was barely debated. In retrospect, that should've been a warning to me. It wasn't heeded.

Instead, I focused on building international influence. The Boards were providing me with what I needed to make the world follow the lead of this country and, without Rana holding me back I was able to bring them around in record time. Our governments worked together to build plans that would bring world economies into a more sustainable future while ensuring that no one was left out in the cold. We built up-lift communities here in the United States, and in many other countries, to make sure people had access to opportunities and, where opportunities were in short supply, to help generate new ones.

Philosophers and economists had aligned before in saying that there would always be haves and have nots and that an economy with winners would also have losers. In a money economy, it was true...but we didn't want a money economy anymore.

America was leading the way toward a future where money was only part of the equation. Peoples' cultural heritage and diversity...that became a currency. The protection of wildlife, that became a goal shared by all.

We built a system where our natural and cultural diversity were money. We built a system where you could benefit more from trying to achieve something sustainable and conscientious than from simply trying to please your customer. Happiness over pleasure: it was a smaller adjustment than I had thought. Before long, the middle eastern oil sheiks were building solar and wind farms. They were working with Europe to preserve Islamic heritage and with China to build a translation of the Quran into an interactive online portal with graphical representations of historical stories. Africa became a hub for emerging technologies through protection investment in their natural beauty. We doubled the number of protected acres. It was really special.

The years fell away. They really do fall away faster the further along you go. But I wasn't about to prove Rana right. I kept The Boards changing things subtly, ensuring people were open to some of the newer ideas Rana and I toyed with but never outright controlling minds. We created safe housing for the homeless and hungry. We legislated independent schooling and offered incentives that lured away professionals in their fields to teach rather than continue pursuing profit for profit's sake. They didn't need to be overwhelming incentives, you see, because the profit motive wasn't the only motive driving the economy anymore. Women and men both found charity and giving back more attractive than self-obsessed creativity or an overabundance of money. Giving back was cool again, maybe for the first time since the Bronze Age, really.

We poured money and resources into medical, environmental, and space research. The orbital platform over Malibu? Got its start there, held aloft by Earth itself and providing enough solar power to light up the whole West Coast. The technology, see, you don't understand. The technology didn't exist...would not have existed...without the road we were on. Rana...I wondered what she would've thought as plans to build orbitals were drafted all over the world. More years passed. The people...they were happy, for the most part. You may have read about the Santa Monica Mountains fire. You were just a child then. It was such a tragedy. I needed to soften it for them. It was nothing to program The Boards to soothe the fears and sorrows of Californians and the people of the US. And that's when I realized it. Rana...she'd seen this day before I did. It isn't always through malice that you become a dictator. Sometimes, it's the heart that bleeds too much for its people, that holds them too closely, that smothers.

I had become the thing I swore I wouldn't.

I looked...out that window, Arbogast. For days, I looked out that window...watching the clouds...watching the green grass grow. I looked out that window looking for a sign...what I found was a plan.

Chapter Twelve

I would come clean.

I'd need to figure out the logistics. I'd need to nudge people into a mental state in which they were prepared...so they were in a mental place where they could hear the facts without disposing of the benefits that mankind had received. For months, I let The Boards do their work. I waited until the behavioral analytics revealed a people ready to hear what I had to say: that I, more than any other leader in the history of the United States, had deceived and manipulated them for years.

I remember the day. The roses were in bloom and the smell was heady, overpowering. I can still smell it, whenever I think back to that moment.

"My fellow Americans and those countries around the world whose partnership we value so highly, I come before you to apologize. While my time here in office has seen an unprecedented period of peace, cooperation, and progress, I must tell you that, at its root, is a lie."

A hush fell over the crowd of reporters. I saw one shed a tear.

"The Boards, those ubiquitous machines that have made their way into every part of our society as advertising, information, and artistic devices, have in fact been feeding all who look at them subtle messages designed to adjust behavior. These messages were never intended to be malicious, in fact, quite the opposite. And it's clear that, while this method is inexcusable, the world has benefited from some of the changes we've made.

Still, the method is inexcusable. You were, without your knowledge, being influenced, controlled.

Of course, I take full responsibility. I started the company that built The Boards. I was a strong proponent of making sure they were everywhere and, when I became aware of what they were doing, I took steps to actively adjust behavior. And to be sure, I stand here today a benefactor of that decision.

Well, no longer. I will not be a party to deceiving you. My plan is to stay and oversee the destruction of The Boards all over the world. I cannot allow another to access the power I, myself, have found too easy to abuse.

To do this, I have already mapped out an aggressive strategy which will be finalized over the coming weeks and executed over the coming year. After this, I will step aside as your President.

At that point, I will face whatever charges the new President feels are appropriate.

I can't imagine how you must feel, hearing this from your President. I can only apologize and take steps to ensure the temptation that lured me is destroyed, never to tempt anyone again. God bless you all."

And with that, I had given it all up. Rana, my friend, had been right all along. I had pushed too far. I could only thank God I'd realized while I was still able to give up the power I had gained.

And then something happened I didn't expect. As my work to destroy The Boards commenced, people's reactions turned from horror to acceptance, to apology and then to action.

Organized marches, write ins, sit ins...all toward one purpose. Keep me in power.

My advisers were telling me to stay and hang on. Then Congress refused to take action against me. One vote for censure.

This reaction didn't make sense, not in any rational way. They should've been outraged. I had expected to have to fight to stay in long enough to shut down The Boards.

What had changed?

Suddenly I was being congratulated for my honesty and the quickness with which I had remedied the situation.

The Boards, I realized, had already worked their magic too well. The people didn't want to ruin what they had...and, in their mind, I was connected to those gains.

This only illustrated the stark reality of the situation. Rana's prediction...an infantilized and weak generation of people...had happened faster than even she'd anticipated.

So I sat in my gilded cage, here, right here, as my name was sung out in celebration, and marveled at the destruction my good intentions had wrought upon our people."

"That's what you think" Arbogast said, waving his gun.

"Oh?"

"You'd like to think that all these people were hypnotized into loving you. Maybe now, with a gun to your head, you can finally admit the truth. You were only fooling yourself."

"Was I?"

Arbogast shifted in his seat and leaned forward, "You are only a man! You can't control everything...The Boards couldn't control everything. That kind of power doesn't exist.

You may have done a lot of damage, but you couldn't fool us all!"

"I never said it did." Teddy said leaning back in his chair.

Arbogast went on, "You couldn't see that, right there in one of your "Uplift Communities" the seeds of your own destruction would be sewn."

"Well, by all means," Teddy said, "enlighten me."

Chapter Thirteen

"My parents...my mom and dad. They clocked what was going on. They'd never liked The Boards. My dad was a Mason, that's a Freemason. He knew something about secret codes and secret influences, and he taught us...from the time I was a child. "Never a free meal...never anything like that from nobody," he used to say. They made sure I could dodge The Boards by home schooling me. They taught me the fear of God and the fear of man when he tries to take too much upon himself.

For a while, like when you're a kid, that's hard to understand. I was home schooled. The only interactions I had with other people were with our own family and friends and with people at the grocery store, which was like my only exposure to The Boards.

I'll admit, when I was a kid, I was fascinated by The Boards. We weren't allowed television either or anything so all we had were some old computers with some private learning material. The only advertising I got were for bible schools and religious school clothing outlets. The only world I knew."

"You must've had a charming childhood." Teddy said as he put his hands up, "I'm sorry but, would you mind if I poured us a whiskey?"

"I grew up with the right kind of people to see the truth. And my parents, they made sure I had friends and community. A community that didn't trust you or The Boards or your whole liberal agenda." Arbogast said, waving the gun side to side and then resting it again, center mass, on Teddy "Get up, pour your whiskey. Anything troubling to me gets a loud answer."

Teddy rose slowly, hands raised. "Trust me, I wouldn't stop this for the world right now," he walked over and dropped some ice into a glass. "Should I pour two?"

"No. I don't drink with confessed murderers." Arbogast smiled wickedly.

"Funny, coming from the man with the gun," he said as he walked back toward the seat with a large whiskey in hand. "Ok, now, you were saying that you didn't trust me or the boards or...the liberal agenda?"

"Yes, none of us did," Arbogast said.

"Even when we funded the faith-based initiatives to get kids off the streets in Little Rock?" Teddy asked.

"You mean when you bought the cooperation of the church in Arkansas with the blood of children?" Arbogast corrected him.

"Sorry, I interrupted you. Please go on." Teddy smiled and sipped at his whiskey.

"I grew up thinking this for the first 17 years of my life.

Then, then...I met a woman.

She changed things, for a while. She opened my mind up to so many possibilities. She seemed so normal. So real. I began to wonder what it was about The Boards that I was so against, anyway. What exactly is a liberal agenda and, if it's so real, what makes it something that we should be against?

I remember the day I told them I was leaving the Spring Rock compound. I was going to marry Sonja. The last day I'd see them, my parents. They disowned me. My mother cried as my father drove me out. He didn't cry, but he embraced me one more time. Then he pushed his Mason ring into my hand, one he'd worn for as long as I could remember, and said "You remember us, boy. Remember us and, maybe someday you'll remember the truth." Then he pushed me out the door, threw some cash at my feet and I never saw them again.

I'd been tainted and those were the rules. They didn't deny forgiveness or epiphany, but they wouldn't abide traitors. They couldn't. Not when your agents were everywhere and your methods so insidious.

I cried too, though I couldn't deny that I had questions about what my father and the compound were teaching. The world didn't seem so bad, especially with Sonja.

Yes, Sonja and her blonde hair were waiting, and I didn't really think anything of being the soldier against the dreaded liberal agenda when I could live a happy life in your golden republic. I went to Sonja. I got a job. I went through life with The Boards all around me. I can't say I paid too much attention to them, but I didn't make any efforts to destroy them or leave them either.

It was good for a while.

Sex, alcohol, and prosperity...a man can go far on that...he can go a long time.

But, of course, prosperity brings choices. And, one day, Sonja chose to leave our little courtship. We'd been engaged for a while...we hadn't set a date. She up and left with a rodeo cowboy, of all things.

Everything hurt, but even then, it wasn't enough to wake me up. I drifted for a while, reading religious texts, smoking pot. I was looking for a wake-up call and I didn't even know it. I stared at my father's ring, marking the details, the scuffs, the wear. I thought of all the meals he cooked and the time he taught me how to ride a bicycle. I thought about the compound and the quiet nights.

Then, it came. That moment of clarity. Right through my mind like an arrow made of diamond, when you got up on television and said what you said.

"I lied to you all...in fact, I'm working on a big liberal agenda and I'm gonna neuter your kids." I'm paraphrasing of course...but the message was clear enough. Mom and Dad were right after all. I was living in sin out here in the world and you...you were king devil in Hell.

I think one eye opened after that. But it was only the beginning. I kept doing my job...working at one of them factories building chips for the de-salinators. Clean water. I wanted to think I was doing a good thing.

I started taking long camping trips. Unplugging myself from your tentacles. I was trying to see what it was like...did I feel different?

I wasn't sure.

Then, it was everywhere all of a sudden. People...groups of people were on the dark net...something you had supposedly shut down. Looks like someone finally had got the drop on you.

I bought a computer and found my way online on the dark net. They had everything you didn't want. Banned media, banned books, banned video games. It was amazing...a whole world I didn't know about. A whole world you kept from us.

Then, I saw it: They Live. An old movie which I wouldn't be surprised if you were familiar with." He paused then, waiting for an indication that Teddy knew.

Teddy smiled "I love that movie. Really all of John Carpenter. Have you seen The Thing?"
"I knew you'd seen it. Your whole lie came from it."
"Now, now...I don't plagiarize...the idea came as I've told you. That you've found similarities is human nature. We find patterns, matches in similar, but not the same, things...that's what we do."
"Don't try to double-talk me." Arbogast said.
"I wouldn't dream of it. Please continue"
"I realized that my mom and dad had given me the special glasses to see...if only I'd put them on. And the dark net...that gave me more. That gave me the chance to meet others just like myself. And I did. So many others. A growing population that had one thing on its mind. Even as the boards came down and you committed yourself to healing the damage that you had done; even as our elected leaders and the vast majority of the sheeple here in this greatest country on earth...even then, a growing number of people had one thing on their mind: Kill Teddy Redhed!

Chapter Fourteen

"Not that anyone said it out loud. Not just yet. At first, it was just a gripe group, just blowing off steam. We worked hard all day and most of us were still subject to the boards in some way. In any case, none of us had any real ambitions to foment rebellion.

Until one user. He showed us so much. None of us liked you...none of us liked what you represent...but he showed us...he showed us PRISM. He broke it all down. Through years of research, he'd given us almost everything you've confessed anyway, though he didn't try to blame so many other people for your brainchild as you have. PRISM was you, start to finish. Don't try to lie your way out of it...And he taught us how to fight back. He was the one who showed us how to mask our internet trail, how to get in touch with like-minded others, how to build and grow an organization."

"And who was this user who had all the answers?" Teddy asked.

"He never gave us his real name. But I suspect you know it." Arbogast remembered the gun and refocused his aim without moving it from his knee where he'd rested it. "After all, you killed him."

Teddy scoffed, "Now...I told you who I've killed. I did kill Rana...but that would've been years and years ago...she's not your rebel leader."

Arbogast frowned, "You know what I mean...you had him killed, one of your deep cover guys. He knew you were on to him at the end...he told us all."

"Well, did you not even get a name?" Teddy asked, "how am I supposed to know who I've supposedly had killed if we don't even have a name to go on?"

"u/Half-Life47...there's the username of the man who, before today is done, will have killed you."

"Arbogast, you really know how to deflate a situation," Teddy looked down at his near empty whiskey, swirled the ice in his glass, "but go on. I'm interrupting again. You were about to tell me more about what this savior of the rebellion did for you."

"Showed us your lies!" Arbogast yelled with indignation.

Teddy put a finger to his lips and then pointed to the door outside. "Careful, careful! You don't want to alert the authorities before you've taken your shot."

Arbogast took a deep breathe, then continued, "Half-Life47 helped us to understand the power of our group and helped us take our first actions. Oddly, it hadn't occurred to us to take action before.

We started by reprogramming some of the boards in our local areas. They were scheduled to come down anyway and, after careful research, we saw that the dismantlers were not checking too closely.

So, we reprogrammed them to generate messages that woke people up. How amazing it was see people questioning more! We watched some local council meetings go from odd harmony to the loud voicing of fears, concerns. We wanted people to make their own minds up! You'd taken it from them...we were giving it back.

Is mutual cooperation and tolerance of other cultures the right way? Is it an invitation for the loudest cultures to defeat the quieter and more reserved ones? When we saw the discord, we had sewn...we knew we'd achieved a victory."

"Congratulations," Teddy said and raised his glass, "you made people afraid of each other. Did it change the policies?"

"No, nothing so drastic. We were just trying to move the needle...but it worked!"

"Did you have an alternative solution to the one they came to?"

"No, and that's *your* problem, you know. There isn't always a solution. Life isn't so clean...we were tired of being told that life was always so clean...we wanted the truth."

"And the truth is that not all problems have perfect solutions?" Teddy asked.

"Yes. No. More than that...some problems don't have solutions at all." Arbogast huffed.

"Anyway, it was a good first test. But we did it in secret. We needed to get out into the world. So, we organized. I became the head of the Southern District. In fact, there was a profile on me on the very first issue of The Brentwood Rebel, that's our online magazine before you ask, where we tell the truth and help people break free of your mind games.

Once we organized, we needed a way to get out into the world. Half-Life47 suggested we hold a rally, but where? I wanted it in Little Rock...but you made sure our state was never covered in the official news anyway, so we decided instead to hold it in New York. We marched down Wall Street. But that was the part that you knew. You must've seen it on the news."

"Yes I did...it had a poor turnout, as I recall," Teddy said, "I'd seen the commentators talking about it."

"Well, what would you expect? President Teddy can't be seen to have a rebellion on his hands... President Teddy wouldn't like it if we covered the truth, so we won't! And anyway...everyone was still plugged into your system."

"I thought The Boards were down by then?" Teddy asked.

Arbogast looked sourly at Teddy, "The damage...the damage was done. You had people ignoring us out of their own accord, so trained were they to do your bidding. So, we tried again in Denver, and again in Los Angeles. We marched, we rallied, we sat in. We blocked highway 5 while you were in town."

Teddy looked mildly amused, "Arbogast, were you there for that?"

"I was, and proud of it," Arbogast smiled.

"You made me hours late for the Russian Federation ambassador."

"If I could've stop you from spewing your poison even for one moment, I'd have considered it a victory."

"Me too! The Russian Federation ambassador is really boring..." Teddy laughed.

"You'll laugh your way into an early grave...but not too early. You need to know...you need to know that we're going to tear it all down."

"Finally, we're getting to the good part."

"I found her in a rally in Memphis...we were tearing down a statue of you. She was just as she had been...though her eyes were tired. But that was because they had been opened. My Sonja...she was holding a rope and pulling you down."

"Wow, really?" Teddy seemed genuinely surprised.

"Not so hard to believe that, once she saw the truth, she would join the rebellion."

"Did you guys end up..." Teddy asked.

"She came back to me when she saw the truth...she realized she was living in a dream world and that I was real. Her one true thing." Arbogast looked into the middle distance for a moment and Teddy supposed he was trying to remember Sonja's face.

"Well, Arbogast, congratulations...you've surprised me."

"Life...my life...was good, for a while. Sonja was back. The Southern district was implementing Half-Life47s ideas quickly and loyally...the other districts were in-step with us. And we were about to move to a plan to start a pirate media broadcast when disaster struck. Half-Life47 discovered he'd been discovered...targeted by you.

You and your truth police were after him, he said, and you were going to get him if he didn't move around.

From then on, we heard less and less of him. While you were implementing your plan to free minds of the effects of The Boards, you were secretly hunting him down.

Left to our own, we drowned in committee. No one could agree on what to do. There were some small protests against the educational seminars and the Post-Board Action Committees but nothing really of note. We'd lost our leader...we were lost.

And then, at Midnight on March 7th, we received one more message from Half-Life47. You'd finally gotten to him. It was chilling...I'll never forget it."

"They're in the house now. I've been betrayed. Trust no one and trust not to nonviolence. Cut off the snake's head and the body dies." Teddy said.

Arbogast's eyes went wide, then hardened, "I see you remember him now." Behind his hard look, injury and fury, just below the surface.

"He strikes a distant chord." Teddy said, looking out the window listlessly.

"And that was where it was born...an operation so secret that no one knows it all...but to make it plain...that's when we decided. We were going to kill Teddy Redhed!

Chapter Fifteen

Everyone had deniability because no one spoke directly about it. We simply decided that it would happen in our own minds and the rest fell into place. We used the old ways...dead letter drops, even Morse code, all off the grid. And that was me! I taught them. I taught them what my parents had taught me. Without ever meeting a soul, we built a new community out of your reach and hatched the plot to end your reign.

I was selected. It was an obvious choice. I had been trained by my father. I would need to carry it out. I want to add to you that I campaigned for it. I wanted it. I wanted to be the one, after all you'd done to humanity."

Teddy interrupted, "You keep saying I'm terrible for humanity. I haven't heard much evidence to support that that I haven't stated myself."

"Pets!" Arbogast shouted, "You'd have us be pets...a world of poodles doing tricks in your yard, waiting for you to beckon. You and your liberal friends want to neuter the human race and make us docile, cooperative, little creatures, always taking the weak way out...forgoing the kind of conflict that makes us strong...that makes us brave...that gives us honor. It's been decades now without a war, so we have no warriors. It's been decades now, where your lie has dominated humanity...and what have we to show for it?"

"A sustainable environment, a peaceful and progress filled world, a people who eat well, care for each other and find some measure of happiness in their lives while they work for an even better world?" Teddy said.

"A prettier doghouse…" Arbogast said.

"Well, can't please everyone…best continue, it's getting late." Teddy said and sat back in his chair.

"I was chosen…but we needed things…I found the gun, some old antiques dealer. That was easy…and access? That's where you really screwed up. I got in here via the tour. Easiest thing in the world.

No, it was the bullets. You regulated bullets a long time ago and that made it hard…but we found a guy. He went by the code name Gannett. That was the one time we had to break the rule…trust no one…but we had to trust him. I had to trust him…I had to meet him. It was dark. It smelled like damp cigarettes…that's the kind of place these deals are done, eh?

A basement in Georgetown…rainy day…the first rainy day in a long time…that's when I met Gannett."

"Gannett?" Teddy asked with a smirk.

"It's not a real name, obviously…what he called himself. He had somehow got hold of a box metropolitan police bullets. We thought he might work in the factory where they're made, some sort of human quality control. Anyway, he had the bullets…and he was the only one, again, thanks to you.

I met him there and he was a nervous one…I couldn't see his face. He kept in the dark and wore some kind of gauze on his face, not that it mattered. He shined a light in my face the whole time, so I couldn't see him.

He said "So you're the patsy…"

I asked him what he meant. He said that a long time ago, people used to think a different liberal president was assassinated by a group who pinned it on one unlucky guy. I told him it wasn't like that...I am going to remove this stain from our great country. From our world. He didn't seem impressed. "Not without my bullets you won't. You can keep dreaming."

I told him we could transfer his fee, in Stellar Lumens, just as requested. But he wanted more...he wanted assurances. "If you're the man to lead us all out of the so-called darkness into a brighter tomorrow. I need something from you...something important."

"What's that?" I asked.

"Something personal...something you'd never part with."

I didn't even carry ID...there was nothing but the cell phone and my clothes...and...

"Yeah," he said, "I think that will do." He'd followed my eyes down to my father's ring.

"You want my ring?"

"Yes. Is that going to be a problem?"

"It belonged to my father. I can't give you that ring."

"See, then there's no deal. This is the thing about revolutionaries...too often they dream of the rewards and too rarely are they ready to make the sacrifice."

"I'm ready!"

"Are you? You're going to die if you take these bullets and load them into whatever gun you got from wherever you got a gun and walk over to the president and try to shoot him. It's not a free world you'll live in. You're deciding to commit suicide by cop."

He was right. I guess I hadn't really let all that sink in. I shut my eyes to the bright light he had in my face and felt sweat creep coldly up my back and wrap around my neck. I was talking like I was still alive. But I wasn't.

"Now you see it, don't you? You're dead either way. If you do it, the best you can hope for is a clean kill from the secret service. If you have to face trial, you'll die slowly...appeals stretching into years behind bars, almost universally hated. On the other hand, now...if you back out...they'll find you. They'll find you and end you before you can rat them out. You're stuck now, boyo."

He stood quietly, breathing through the gauze on his face. I wondered how he coped with all that on his face in this dark and why he bothered. The light was blinding.

I felt the cold sweat creep up my back as I slipped off the ring, squeezed it in my hand, handed it to him.

"There we are! See, now that wasn't so hard...a life for a life. And I'll even make you a deal. If you get through all this...I'll see you get it back if I can. If not? Well, I'll have a high value trinket...creeps love this short of shit."

I felt heady...light.

"The box of ammunition is under the red brick stacked on two cinder blocks just outside the door. Take them and go. And you'll note, there are three bullets missing. Those are the bullets for you and your closest associates. I'll use them if I don't get my money, so you just make that transfer, boyo."

The light went out and I was alone.

I sat in the darkness, underground, for a long time...feeling the gravity, the moment. I breathed in the darkness, the sweat, the smoke of a thousand dead butts sinking beneath my feet.

When I surfaced, I wasn't just some crackpot playing around online, I wasn't a grass roots opposition leader, I wasn't a rebel. I was Arbogast, the executioner."

Arbogast leveled the gun at Teddy's Chest.

"So, Teddy," Arbogast smiled, "any last words?"

Teddy looked at the muzzle of the gun and gulped. Real fear crept into his eyes for just a moment, or was it resignation? Arbogast couldn't tell.

"I have, maybe, one more confession to make...before you...do me in."

"And what is that?" Arbogast asked.

Teddy put his hands up and slowly put his hand to his jacket lapel. He opened his jacket slowly and then looked back at Arbogast "I'm going to reach into my pocket, don't do anything stupid. There's no panic button, no weapon...look you can see...I have something to show you."

"Slowly. Even if you hit a panic button now, it won't stop you from dying." Arbogast said, raising the gun and closing one eye to aim.

Teddy put his hand into his pocket and slowly pulled it out again, closed. Then, he placed a small object down on the coffee table between them that made a tapping sound against the glass top. Arbogast looked down and saw it and gasped.

It was his father's ring.

Chapter Sixteen

"You son of a bitch. You killed Gannett?"

"No, Arbogast," Teddy said calmly, "But you're about to. You're pointing a gun at Gannett, boyo."

Arbogast sat quietly, his head shaking from side to side in small, tense jerks. "I don't,"

"Of course you don't." Teddy, said, still very calm.

Arbogast was quiet for a long while. Teddy could hear his breathing. When he spoke, Arbogast could only whisper "Why?"

"What was that?" Teddy said, "I didn't get that."

"Why?" Arbogast said, finding his voice and meeting Teddy's eyes.

"The why...yeah, well, I guess we have a bit of time...as a matter of fact, Arbogast, I know we do. There's no reason for you to worry. There are no more meetings today. My schedule is clear. Do you mind if I get another drink?" And Teddy slowly got to his feet and poured himself a glass.

Arbogast found his voice after a while, "You couldn't have. No, this is a lie. Gannett...was he working for you? Was it a sting?"

Teddy took on an intensity that he hadn't shown all night, "No, no, no! Arbogast! You can't go backward now, not now! We need you right here. I was Gannett! You look at that ring. I couldn't have gotten it this fast any other way. Come on now, Arbogast, stay with me!"

Arbogast was thrown off, looking almost as if he might faint.

"Come on now buddy," Teddy took a gentler tone, "we can get through this. Here, have a drink. You look like you need it."

Arbogast repointed the gun at Teddy, "Sit down!"

Teddy smiled, dropped an ice cube into his drink and sat back down. Arbogast steadied himself, then said "Now! Tell me exactly...why?"

"Well," Teddy started, "where did we leave in my story...oh yes, I was sitting in a cage. This cage...and the metaphorical cage I'd built myself. I had made people work well together...I had paused the ferocity of the human race just long enough to save them from disaster but, in doing so, I had made them docile.

Welcome to the world of imperfect solutions, am I right?

I stared out the window here for so long...wondering what to do. I sat in this office and signed papers and tried to walk back much of the damage I'd done...but people just weren't cooperating. Even after The Boards were coming down, people were ready to acquiesce to me...to follow my lead. What would happen wouldn't be the clean and easy recovery I originally anticipated...what was being born of this was a new arms race. The first people to come out of the trance would swing hard right and could even try for world domination. Would that be the legacy of all this progress? A stronger and more lasting world that suffocated under the rule of an angry dictator?

Even if nothing like that happened. People who only follow and don't think for themselves will one day, somehow, fall into ruin.

And then it came to me. If I could control the creation of this state, I could manage its deconstruction.

Not with The Boards, they were already going away, and we had just destroyed the PRISM site and backup sites. Not by manipulating the masses...Rana was a ghostly conscience, making certain I could never take that path again.

But in a smaller population, maybe. Maybe I could foment some dissent.

I'd have to be careful, but the plan was already forming.

After a few months, I knew I needed just one person. Not alone...there had to be a few others, but you'd be surprised how few it takes to lend the flavor of revolution to an online conspiracy. I worked in the residence mainly...dropping material in the one place I knew would attract the element I needed: the dark net. By the way, you might've found it easy to believe anything you read from me on the dark net. You know why? The Boards. I took them down off the regular internet as promised...but the dark net was restricted, Arbogast. Naughty, naughty of you to be looking at it in the first place. What do you expect out there with the thieves and the black market?

Selling all of you on revolution reminded me of the old days, actually...selling businesses on data solutions. When I had a decent sized number of regular viewers, I did some discreet background checks on all of them.

But when I found you, I knew I had my man. You were selected. It was an obvious choice. You'd been trained by your father and, also, you had all the intrinsic qualities necessary, misanthropy, paranoia. You have the profile, Arbogast, the history, everything...you, my beautiful and ultimate patsy.

In short order, you knew me as Half-Life47. I set you, and the others, some small tests. But I knew from the first, it would be you sitting there in front of me right now."

"You're a liar!" Arbogast shouted, eyes wide and watery.

"I'm an actor! To be sure, a good actor may deceive, but is that the same thing as lying?"

"You couldn't have been Half-Life47!"

"And why not? Had you met him? Did you even get a positive ID on the gender of Half-Life47?" Teddy waited for a moment to see if Arbogast had an answer.

Arbogast felt the venom rise within him. He wanted to spew it out...he felt the trigger under his finger, felt his finger tighten ever so slightly. Through clenched teeth, he said "Go on."

"I gave you some simple tasks. Of course, you could never have achieved anything real, other than let some people know that other people did have different opinions. Part of me hoped that would do the trick and we could all go home. But most of me knew, that wasn't going to make the difference. I had offended nature, Arbogast. In my arrogance, I had created a monster. Now, to kill that monster, a sacrifice was demanded. But I get ahead of myself. I expected you to rise up the leadership ranks but, it turns out, you didn't have as much administrative ability as I'd hoped. Arbogast, you're all heart. I want you to know it wasn't I who held you back in the organized opposition. It was the leadership that had elected themselves. And you went along with it, like a lamb. We hate the things we become, no? Or is it the other way around? I'm not sure.

In the end, I engineered a quick exit when it seemed appropriate and let the boards do their work on your little conclave, leaving you with a quote steeped in the imagery and history that will resonate with people of your particular upbringing: Cut off the head and the snake will die.

And the boards worked to keep that message at the forefront of your minds...to translate and interpret it for you...to tell you what you had to do. To tell you what you really wanted. After all, you really want to Kill Teddy Redhed!

Chapter Seventeen

"I don't believe it!" Arbogast shouted.

"That's ok." Teddy said.

"I don't believe you!" Arbogast shouted.

"That's ok." Teddy said.

Arbogast stared down at his father's ring, unable to avoid the clear picture it brought into focus.

All this time, had he really been maneuvered into this? He had been free. He had been set free!

There was no reason why he should believe this. But that ring. His father's ring.

"You don't look so sure, Arbogast. You look like you don't know what to believe anymore."

"Why..." he said, "Why, if you knew that I was going to come and kill you?"

Teddy was up again, pouring himself another drink. This time, he poured one for Arbogast. Setting the drink down in front of him, he said "I'd have thought that was relatively obvious from the story I told, but I'm glad it's not because now I can tell you, instead, the way I look at it."

Teddy sat quietly for a moment and sipped from his glass, then, "You know, I haven't been drunk in a great, long while. I stopped drinking, mostly, a while back. I find that, now...I relish the feeling.

But you want an answer to your question. Here it is. I am not going to make decisions anymore for the people. You are or, rather, we are."

Arbogast's eyes snapped up to meet Teddy's, "What?"

"Well, here it is! This is it. The culmination of all the plans. You, in that chair, with that gun and one important choice. You can kill me, or you can leave. If you kill me, you will complete a plan I set in motion years ago. You will also seal your fate.

You could also leave. If you do that, we will both go on, though you will of course suffer a long prison sentence for conspiring to kill the President. The key about this is that, while I've maneuvered you to this point...the choice now, is all yours.

Arbogast shook his head, "If what you say is true...and you truly planned all of this out...if you've truly manufactured this moment, then I can't believe you would leave anything to chance."

"And why not?" Teddy responded, "If there's a lesson in all of this, isn't it that a world too well planned leaves no room for the spontaneity of the human experience? If one man assumes he can see all ends and the world agrees with them, then we're all blind, isn't that it?"

"You said that to me once, as Half-Life47," Arbogast said, staring at the ring.

Teddy smiled as he noted Arbogast's resignation to the truth, "I also told you I'd return the ring to you. There it is. You could put it on and walk away."

"Was that the plan?" Arbogast asked, glumly.

"No! No plan, not in this moment, just a choice."

Arbogast reached down and grabbed the ring and slid it onto his finger. He felt the cold metal against his skin. He felt his father's words. He felt Sonja's hair on his chin, tickling. He remembered the feeling of falling off a bicycle, suddenly. He snapped to attention and looked at Teddy. "What happens?" he asked, "What happens?"

"What do you mean?" Teddy said.

"You said I have a choice...so what happens in either case?"

Teddy smiled, "Yes! That's excellent. That's why you're the one to make the choice. You're not that bright and not that strong, Arbogast, I hope you don't mind my saying...but you are human, through and through."

"What happens!" Arbogast shouted.

"Well...if you kill me." Teddy set his glass down to better use his hands when he talked. He seemed oddly animated and Arbogast thought he might be a little drunk. "If you kill me...well...you create a martyr."

"A martyr?"

"Yes. I become a martyr to the policies and reforms I've set in place. The modeling suggests that you'd set in motion another 100 years of progressive reforms and policy adherence that would be set against a gradual resumption of independence and differences. I die, the world gets to continue in toward a big, bright, beautiful tomorrow, based on mutual respect and peace. When differences surface, and they will, it'll be a long time before anyone starts a war over them.

It's bad news for me but the world you want to usher in with this violent act, one where only the strong have a voice; where war, not discourse, bring glory; where wealth and not mercy is the cornerstone of success, where pleasure sits on the throne only happiness can truly satisfy...or what you might call the good old days...will never happen. Meanwhile, it's bad news for you. You'll be kept alive long enough for the world to, for the first time in a long time now, unite against a common enemy.

They will commit a wanton act of violence and kill you after a long trial. People will, if I do say so myself, be heartbroken and revenge will be slow, painful and memorable. In fact, it will stick in their collective unconscious and start a process of unwinding what I have done with The Boards."

"And if I let you live?" Arbogast asked.

Teddy sighed, "If you put that gun down, men will be here in moments to put you in prison. I win, in a way, because I live. The world loses a bit...as the secret service won't let this stunt happen again and my death from old age, even if I'm not re-elected, will not have the effect needed to shock people out of their repressed state. You, actually, will live. I'll do everything I can to keep you safe, in prison of course. I'll speak eloquently on the power of forgiveness. You may even live long enough to see the world collapse under the weight of an oppressive dictator, some aberration that will inevitably wake up and realize I've left world ripe for the picking. As I said, this is your choice."

Arbogast reached for the drink and drained the glass. He looked at the ring on his finger and wondered, not for the first time today, what his father would've have done in his place.

Teddy tapped on the table, "But that's the great thing about choice, isn't it? I could be wrong about all of this. You only have my models to go on. The choice is yours."

"What do you want me to do?" Arbogast asked.

Teddy said forcefully, with more than a hint of annoyance, "Would you be commanded by me now? After swearing yourself to be my executioner for the very reason that I have come to dominate the world with my "liberal agenda"?"

Arbogast scoffed, "I didn't say it would command my decision."

"Well, I'm not making it that easy. You've got this one...boyo. You're the one with the gun. You've come this far. Is your world worth dying for?"

"Yes, of course," Arbogast spat.

"Yes, of course!" Teddy sang back at him, "So here we are with a decision to make then!"

"You want me to kill you." Arbogast said.

"Do I?"

"You said you stopped drinking, tonight you're getting drunk."

"It seemed like a good time," Teddy said, "as I've got a gun to my head."

"You set all this in motion...you planned for me to come here, gun in hand."

"Yes, I've done all that." Teddy said.

"You gave me...you even gave me the bullets." Arbogast said.

"Yes. It would be reasonable to suspect that I want you to kill me."

Arbogast looked down at the eagle image woven into the rug. Looked at the bunch of arrows clutched in its talons. "I should make you live in your golden cage. You've planned this, all this. Right up to this conversation. I don't understand it all, but I know you shouldn't be trusted."

"Well then, by all means, put down your gun. I will call the secret service and you can spend your days watching the world we built together falling apart. We both will," Teddy said, "each within our respective prison cells."

"Getting cold feet?" Arbogast asked.

"Not at all. This must be what it is. I cannot make you pull that trigger or put that gun down. I've not programmed you. It'll come down to a choice. A real choice. Either way, Arbogast, whatever choice you make, you will commit the original sin that births a new world." Arbogast felt the liquor pounding at his temples. He was sweating now; his palms were wet. He felt the pain of terrible decision upon him. He'd been trapped, he realized now. He was playing Teddy's game, and whichever move he made, he couldn't be sure what would happen next. Only Teddy knew. Did Teddy know? He felt a surge of grief. He wanted to drop the gun and run through the window. He felt his heart pound. "You...you..." he huffed.

"Me, Arbogast, what will you do about me?" Arbogast felt the words lash at his face. He felt vacant, like parts of his mind were going dark. He felt his finger relax against the trigger. His head, swimming with doubt, tears welled up in his eyes.

He struggled to think what his father would do, what the leader of his rebellion would've done...what would Half-Life47 have done?

Teddy opened his mouth to speak but there was a loud wrapping on the door.

Shocked into action, Arbogast tightened his finger on the trigger and an explosion cut through the burdens weighing on his brain. The smell of iron filings...the smoke. Teddy dropped to the ground, writhing and grabbing at his chest.

A blood curdling scream rang out as the doors burst open. The secret service rushed in and tackled Arbogast. He could see himself being pushed onto the ground as if he was outside his body. He hardly felt the knee in his back. His eyes were locked wide open, staring at Teddy Redhed, President, gurgling and dying on the carpet.

Another black suited secret service man came in and checked his pulse, screamed for the secretary to call the medic. Teddy stopped grasping at his chest. His hands lay at his sides, twitching gently.

Arbogast stared on in horror, his hands being bound as a knee pressed hard into his back, threatening to break his ribs.

What had Teddy said? "A choice." What had he done?

Then Teddy's hand went up and pointed. He whispered something to the secret service man kneeling over him. The man in the suit seemed to argue for a moment but the hand went to his shoulder and the man capitulated. He lifted Teddy, who gasped and choked as his head was lifted toward Arbogast.

"Arbogast...Arbogast...now...it's our world." He smiled and Arbogast could see the blood filling Teddy's mouth. The medic rushed in and started examining the wound and then calling out for a stretcher. He held pressure on the wound.

"I'm sorry...I'm sorry, Arbogast...I'm..." Then he was quiet.

The man pressing on Teddy's wound slowed, sagged. The man holding him said, "Oh my god."

Arbogast watched the scene with no sound. He watched one of the men struggle to his feet and run for the door. Near the door, in the corner of his vision, the secretary was red faced and sobbing. The pounding of blood in Arbogast's ears made him hot. He wanted to take his shirt off all of a sudden. It didn't make sense to him, for a moment, that he couldn't.

The rush of realization was almost too much for him and he made a sound, or imagined he did. President Theodore Redhed, President of the United States for about as long as Arbogast had been alive was lying dead by his hand. He had, finally, done what he came to do. And, truly, he felt the bittersweet elation that he had imagined he would. There was a fire now, lit in the hearts and minds of people. He could see it now. He could finally see the picture that Teddy had seen. The choice Arbogast had made, in all it's terrible glory.

He was going to die, just as Teddy had predicted. He was going to die after a long drawn out trial...so much hate and venom. The world would kill him. They would smile as they did it...then realize how much they had lost in the act. They would betray themselves in a fit of rage and loss.

That would lead to a distrust of the human condition in general and, while that distrust would be hard to register at first, it would grow in time into a diversity of choice that would lead to a less harmonious, but healthier human race.

Teddy had seen, as Arbogast knew now, that the human race needed that diversity because the challenges facing humanity would require more than one vision to solve.

The bullet he'd sent into Teddy's heart set in motion the unwinding of the brainwashing...the psychological atrophy The Boards had instilled. It had to be Arbogast's choice. It had to be their world.

He knew then that Teddy had only been acting to bring about the world he thought was right. He had been wrong, and he had given his life to correct his mistake.

Arbogast knew and, more than this, he knew no one else would believe him. Arbogast had destroyed the only other who knew. At that moment, he would've given anything to have a little more time with Teddy Redhed. Time enough to thank him. To thank him for the sacrifice he was making for the world. Arbogast wanted to tell Teddy that, finally, he understood.

Instead, he cried. He cried out into the new world. He cried, and cried, and cried.

The End

ISBN-13: 9798416791063